Cute as a button

by Carrie Hennon

Licensed exclusively to Top That Publishing Ltd
Tide Mill Way, Woodbridge, Suffolk, IP12 1AP, UK
www.topthatpublishing.com
Copyright © 2015 Tide Mill Media
All rights reserved
4 6 8 9 7 5 3
Manufactured in China

Written by Carrie Hennon
Illustrated by Gareth Llewhellin

ISBN 978-1-78445-372-5

A catalogue record for this book is available from the British Library

For the cutest buttons I know - Joshua and Phoebe.
With love from Auntie Carrie. x

My Mummy had a big, round tummy.
It got bigger every day.
Mummy told me my little brother or sister was inside.
Daddy said Mummy was keeping baby safe and warm.

One morning,
when I woke up,
Grandma and Grandpa
were waiting downstairs.
Mummy and Daddy had gone
to the hospital in the night.

'Baby is on the way,' said Grandpa.

I waited and waited for baby ...
but babies take a long time!
I played with my toys but
they were no fun.

Then Daddy rushed in
with a big smile on his face.
'You have a baby sister,' he said,
'and she's as cute as a button!'

'Cute as a button?' I thought.

'What does Daddy mean?'

Later, at bathtime,
Daddy played boats with me.

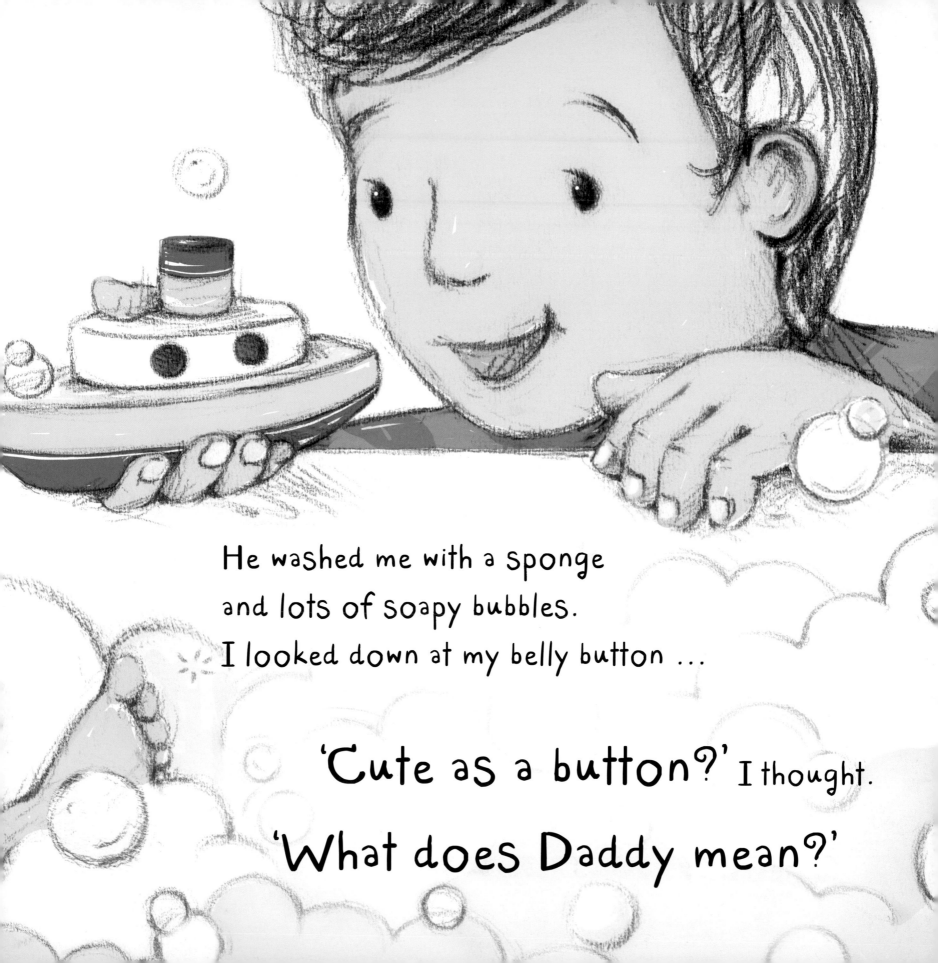

He washed me with a sponge
and lots of soapy bubbles.
I looked down at my belly button ...

'Cute as a button?' I thought.

'What does Daddy mean?'

The next morning
at breakfast time,
Daddy was talking
on the telephone.

He was smiling and laughing.
'She's as cute as a button!'
he said.

'Cute as a button?'
I thought.

'What does Daddy mean?'

'What's cute
about buttons?'
I wondered.

I looked at the buttons on the
clothes in the washing basket.
They didn't look cute.

I looked at the buttons on the
washing machine. They had flashing
lights - but they didn't look cute.

I looked at the television buttons.
I pressed them all at once,
and there was a funny noise ...
but they didn't look cute.

Then I looked in Mummy's tin of buttons. There were lots and lots of buttons, all the colours of a rainbow. Maybe one of these buttons was cute.

But none of them looked cute to me.

Grandma and Grandpa came to visit again.
'We've been to see Mummy,' Grandpa said,
'and we've met your sister.'
'She's as cute as a button!' Grandma said.

'Cute as a button?' I thought.

'What does Grandma mean?'

I didn't understand ...
How could my baby sister be as cute as a button?
I couldn't find anything cute about buttons at all!

Then, **yippee!** Daddy brought Mummy home.
Mummy was carrying a bundle all wrapped in a blanket.
She bent down to show me what was inside.
I stretched up on tiptoe to see ...

a tiny round face ...

big shiny eyes ...

soft dimpled cheeks ...

I smiled at my baby sister
and said ...

'You really are as cute as a button!'